surprise for robin

by Jeanette Perkins Brown

drawings by Dorothy Papy

SURPRISE
FOR
ROBIN

BY JEANETTE PERKINS BROWN

DRAWINGS BY DOROTHY PAPY

FRIENDSHIP PRESS NEW YORK

FORMAT BY DOROTHY PAPY

LIBRARY OF CONGRESS CATALOG CARD NUMBER 56—9250

Robin kissed her mother and ran down to the gate. Her
best friend Yukiko and her mother were waiting to take
her to kindergarten.

Robin bowed to Yukiko's mother. She had been living
so long in Japan that she did as her Japanese friends did.
She spoke as they spoke—in Japanese.

"Good morning," she said politely, though she was in
a hurry to tell them something.

Then she said, "We are going home to America! We are going next week."

The corners of Yukiko's mouth turned down. "I don't want you to go away," she said to Robin.

Robin took her hand, and they walked along without saying anything.

Down the street Seiji was waiting to join them. He had a pet beetle in a little bamboo cage.

"See my beetle?" he asked. He hardly listened when Yukiko told him Robin was going away.

He went right on talking about his beetle and his cage. "It is the very best kind of cage there is," he said. "It has a special door." He let Robin carry it a little way.

"It is the prettiest cage I ever saw," she said when she gave it back.

On the kindergarten porch stood their teacher. Robin and Yukiko bowed to her while Seiji went around to the morning glories. He wanted to show them to his beetle.

"Robin is going to America," said Yukiko to the teacher.

"I brought my book of pictures," Robin said, "to show

where I live in America. I have pictures of my school, too."

"Will you show them to us after our morning song?" the teacher asked. "It is time to go in now."

Before they went inside, the children changed their shoes for soft slippers.

The children were in their circle. They bowed their heads for a song:

> The bright clear morning,
> The still, lovely evening,
> Our food and clothes, too,
> All are gifts from our heavenly Father.

Now they were ready to hear about Robin's book. She
showed them the cover, which had a picture of a big ship.
"This is the ship we came on to Japan," she told them.
"It had a playroom for children."

"You should have come in an airplane," said Seiji. "It is quicker."

"We had too many trunks to go on an airplane," Robin explained, and she turned the page. The first picture showed Robin's home in America. Her baby sister was in a play pen in the yard.

"Look! The baby is in a cage!" the children said.

"It is like my cage, only bigger," Seiji said.

Robin laughed. "That is her play pen," she said. "The baby is safe in a play pen. She can't crawl to the street where she might get hurt."

"Why doesn't your mother carry her baby on her back the way our mothers do?" Yoko wanted to know. "That is the safest place for the baby."

"It is just a different custom," said the teacher, and Robin turned the page.

"Here is my nursery school in America," said Robin. "See me on top of the slide?"

"Just like ours," said Taro. "I like to climb the ladder and slide down again."

"I could climb even a higher one," Seiji boasted.

"This is my church," said Robin. "I went to the nursery room. Next year I will be in the primary room."

"The people are going into the church with their shoes on!" Yoko exclaimed in surprise. "Why don't they take them off at the door as we do?"

"It is just a different custom," said Robin, turning the page.

The next page showed Robin on a picnic.

"Where are your chopsticks?" someone asked, and Robin explained, "We do not eat with chopsticks. We use forks and spoons in America."

"You have funny customs," said Seiji. "Did you have a pet beetle?"

"I had a kitty," said Robin. "Here is her picture."

When Robin left the room to get a drink of water, the teacher said, "We will miss Robin. What can we do before she goes to show that we are her friends?"

"We can give her presents," Yukiko answered.

"You could take pictures of us with your camera so she will have a book about Japan," suggested Michi.

"We can find pretty leaves for it, too," said Taro.

"We can fold paper ships for her," Haruko said.

"I am going to give her a doll," Yukiko said, "because Robin is my best friend."

Seiji said nothing, but he frowned as if he were thinking. Seiji liked to be different.

When the children folded squares of paper into little ships, Seiji folded his into an airplane. When the others painted pictures of flowers for Robin, Seiji painted a picture of his beetle in its little wooden cage.

"It's the best kind of cage there is," he said proudly, "with a special door."

The next day the class went on a picnic walk to find pretty leaves and take pictures. As they went they sang:

Hand in hand on a country road
We walk, and our shoes make a squeaking.
We play we're a flock of little birds,
And our shoes are making a chirping.

When they found a place to stop, they put down their lunches and played games. They had a hopping race first.

Next they played Cat and Mouse. Robin got down on her hands and knees and said to the teacher, "Please take a picture of me being a mouse!" Then she squealed and tried to run, for Seiji was a cat chasing her!

After the games they opened their lunch boxes and took out their chopsticks. Their food was in little pans just large enough to hold some rice and fish and a vegetable. Robin's vegetable was green beans.

The teacher took another picture while they were eating. Seiji made a funny face just as the shutter clicked.

After lunch the children began to look for leaves—all but Seiji.

"We will find the very prettiest for you," they told Robin—all but Seiji.

Seiji was looking for something in the tree bark.

"He is looking for a beetle to race with his," said Taro.

When Seiji joined them, he had a broad smile on his face and another beetle in his cage.

The next two days the children were busy pressing some of the leaves and making leaf prints of others.

"They will make a nice book for Robin," they said. Robin was pleased. "I will show them to all my friends in America," she promised.

Seiji was trying to make a cage for the extra beetle. First he tried paper strips, but they let the beetle through. Then he tried little twigs, but they broke. He punched holes in a small box, but it did not look like a cage. It was hard to make a cage as pretty as his little bamboo one.

Then came Robin's last day at the kindergarten. It was full of surprises. All her Japanese friends seemed to have presents for her. Yukiko brought her a doll.

Michi gave her a coloring book with Japanese pictures.

Haruko gave her a book showing how to fold paper into toys, with a package of folding paper inside it.

Shinko gave her a box of crayons.

Yoshiko gave her a little pin made like a parasol.

Aiko gave her a fan with a picture on it.

Taro brought her a pair of wooden shoes like those that he wore.

Seiji looked very happy for some reason. He did not hand Robin a present, but his eyes danced as if he had a secret. And when no one was looking, he slipped something into Robin's lunch box.

Robin's arms were full of presents, and her face was full of smiles. "All these surprises," she said happily when her mother came for her, "from all my friends!"

But it was not until she emptied her lunch box at home that she discovered the biggest surprise of all.

"Oh, Mommie!" she cried. "Seiji gave me a beetle, AND HIS SPECIAL LITTLE CAGE WITH A DOOR!"

"How very kind of Seiji!" exclaimed her mother. But then she looked troubled.

"The cage is beautiful," she said. "It will always remind you of Seiji. But, darling, the beetle's home is in Japan. He is used to these trees, and he knows how to find his own kind of food here. We could not take him to America."

Robin puckered her forehead. She sat very still. She had to think.

"I know," she said at last, jumping up. "I will leave him with Yukiko! She is my best friend, and he can live in her garden."

So Robin left her beetle in Yukiko's garden the day she went away.

Robin took all her presents on the ship with her when she left for America. She carried the little cage herself.

"It is the best kind of cage there is," she said. "It has a special door, and Seiji gave it to me. I am going to keep my best treasures in it always."